T0197605

the Adventures of Snook and Gator

too many bad ideas

Written and Illustrated by:

Tara Annette Rocker

To order additional copies of this book, contact:
Xlibris
844-714-8691
www.Xlibris.com
Orders@Xlibris.com

ISBN: Softcover   978-1-4415-6590-7
        EBook   978-1-5035-4911-1

Print information available on the last page

Rev. date: 09/02/2022

Devoted to my Mama, Dad, and big Sister
Thanks for letting me be a kid, band-aids and all.

It was a bright and sun shinning day in Bay Point and Snook decided to play outside in her backyard.

"Gator I am going to swing as high and fast as I can!"

Snook decided to try some super tricks while she was swinging.
"Look Gator! I can swing with one hand!"

Snook decided to try an even more super trick.

"Look at me Gator! No hannnds!!!!"

"AUGH!!!"

Snook fell so fast she could not grab the swing in time.

Gator rushed over to sniff Snook, making sure she was okay.

"I'm okay Gator, but that was a bad idea."
Snook said while crying.

Snook's Mama heard her cry and gave Snook a bag of ice for her head.

Mama also gave Snook a hug and kiss.

"You need to play safe Snook." Mama said.

Snook decided to ride her bike.

Snook was in such a hurry to ride her bike that she forgot her helmet.

As soon as she hopped on the bike she began making motorcycle noises.

"Brmmmmm . . . brmmm!" Snook growled.

Snook stopped making motorcycle noises and decided to ride her bike with no hands.

Snook thought she looked pretty cool.

CRASH!!!

Snook was having so much fun she did
not see the bump in the road.

Over the handle bars Snook flew.
Over and over she rolled.

"Ouch! Ow! Waaa!"

Snook ran into the house crying.

Mama could not look at Snook's cuts and scrapes.

So she asked Snook's big sister, Sissy to clean her up.

Sissy gently cleaned Snook's cuts and put on band aids.

Sissy gave Snook's head a pat and said,

"That was a bad idea Snook."

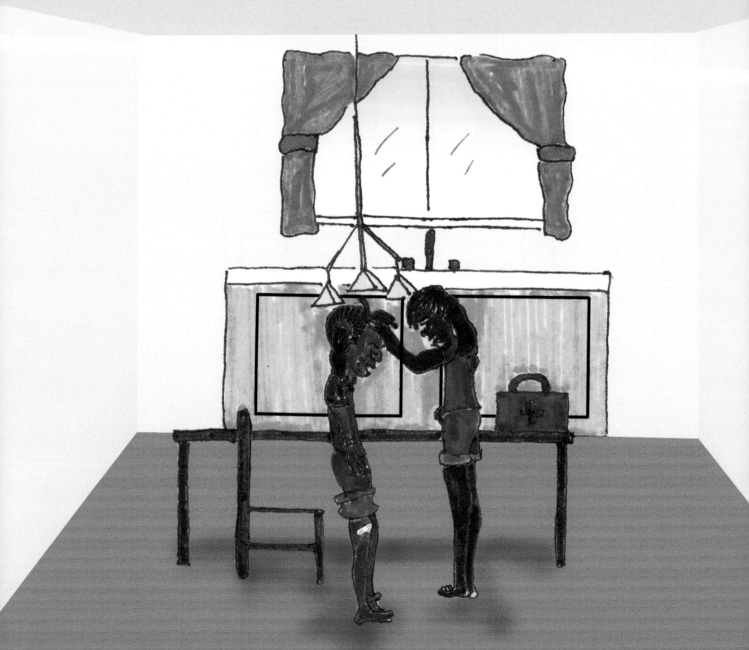

Snook decided to return to the backyard and play cowgirl.

Snook imagined that she was in the Wild West.

In the distance Snook spots an outlaw.

Off she runs!

Snook decided to pretend that Gator is a real horse.

Snook climbed onto Gator's back. Gator whined.

"I am a cowgirl!" Snook yelled.

"Let's go Gator!" Snook shouted.

Gator ran fast, then suddenly stopped.

"AUGH!!!!"

Snook went flying off Gator's back.

"I'm so sorry Gator. That was a bad idea."

Now it is time for a nap.

"Mama said I had too many bad ideas today."

Auto Biography

I was born in Bay Point, California. I was raised by parents with a Southern influence. The Adventures of Snook and Gator are based on the fun and imagination I had as a child.

Printed in the United States
by Baker & Taylor Publisher Services